Mrs. F.

READ ALL THESE

NATE THE GREAT

DETECTIVE STORIES

BY MARJORIE WEINMAN SHARMAT

WITH ILLUSTRATIONS BY MARC SIMONT:

Nate the Great Saves The King of Sweden

by Marjorie Weinman Sharmat
illustrations by Marc Simont

Delacorte ▦ Press

Published by
Delacorte Press
Bantam Doubleday Dell Publishing Group, Inc.
1540 Broadway
New York, New York 10036

Library of Congress Cataloging-in-Publication Data
ISBN 0-385-32120-1
Cataloging-in-Publication Data is available from the Library of Congress.

The text of this book is set in 18-point Goudy Old Style.
Book design by Julie E. Baker

Manufactured in the United States of America
November 1997
10 9 8 7 6 5 4 3 2 1

This book is dedicated to the
King of Sweden,
who, would you believe,
I do not know,
but I think I would like to know,
provided he is grateful
that I kept Rosamond
from knocking on his palace door.
                                    —M.W.S.

I, Nate the Great, am a detective.
My dog, Sludge, helps me.
I solve easy cases and hard cases.
Sometimes I solve strange cases.
Especially for Rosamond.
But this summer Rosamond was
in Scandinavia.
There would not be any
strange cases to solve.
That is what I, Nate the Great,
thought until I looked
in my mailbox.

1

I found a big picture postcard
from Rosamond.
The picture was of a palace.
So far, so good.
There was a message from
Rosamond.

Dear Nate,
I was in Norway.
Now I am in Sweden.
I was in this palace today.
I did not see the king.
I did not see a detective.
I lost something on my trip.
I don't know where.
I need your help.
If you don't help me,
I will have to ask

the King of Sweden
to take the case.

                Rosamond

P.S. What I lost is very tiny
and works only at night.
It lives in dark places.
It looks smart like you
and thinks hard like you
but it has a very long nose
so it probably thinks
through its nose
instead of its head
but I'm not sure about that.

Rosamond was even stranger
in Scandinavia
than she was at home.

I, Nate the Great,
could not take a case
that was thousands
and thousands
and thousands
of miles away.
I threw Rosamond's card
in the wastebasket.

The next day I got another card.

Here are the rules:
If you don't take the case,
call Sweden. Ask for Rosamond.
If you take the case,
you don't have to call.
                    Rosamond
P.S. If you don't take the case,
I will hire that king.
I will call him up.
I will send him cards.
I will knock on his palace door.
I will get him.

I stared at Rosamond's card.
There was a nice stamp on it.
There was a man's picture on the stamp.

He looked like a king.
He did not look like anyone
who would want to be hired
by Rosamond.
I began to think.
This could be my biggest case yet.
It was international.

Rosamond had lost something
in a foreign country.
Maybe in a palace.
Maybe I could even save
the King of Sweden
from Rosamond.
I wrote a note to my mother.

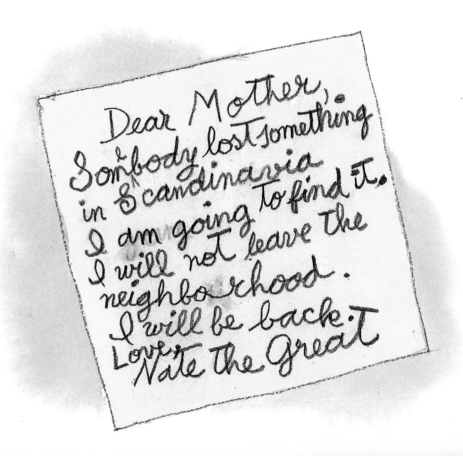

This case was a big blank.
Rosamond had not sent her address.
I did not know what she lost
or when she lost it
or what country she lost it in.
How could I even begin?
I decided to start at Annie's house.
Annie and Rosamond are good
friends.
Sludge and I went to Annie's house.
Annie was out front
with her dog, Fang.
"I am on a case," I said.
"Rosamond lost something
somewhere in Scandinavia.
What do you know about
her trip?"

"I helped her pack," Annie said.

"What did she pack?" I asked.

"Was it anything that looked smart
and had a long nose?"

Fang looked up.

He thought I was talking about him.

Annie said, "Rosamond took
clothes, shoes,
boots for hiking in the mountains,
toothbrush and paste,
a hairbrush,
and toys for her cats."
"Rosamond took her cats to
Scandinavia?"
"Yes, she said that the fish
taste better over there."
"What she lost does not sound like
anything that she packed."
"She packed in a strange way,"
Annie said. "She had a special
place for everything.
She put her left boot
on the left side of her suitcase,

and her right boot on the right side.
She put her cats' toy mice in
her shoes."
"Why?"
"She said her shoes could be
like mice holes for the mice.
Their home. Want to hear more?"
"Not if I can help it," I said.

12

"Tell me, has Rosamond written
to you?"
"Well, last week I got
this photo from Norway."
Annie pulled a picture
from her pocket.
I looked at it.
I saw Rosamond and her four cats.
They were standing in front
of a store.
It looked like a gift shop.
There were T-shirts and mugs
and little figures
in the store window.
Rosamond and her cats
were all wearing T-shirts.

Printed on every shirt was
NORGE KJERLIGHET ROSAMOND.
I turned the picture over.
On the back Rosamond had written,
"This means Norway Loves Rosamond."
Annie said, "Rosamond told me
that she was going to buy

T-shirts and have something
printed on them."
"Aha!" I said. "Since Rosamond
didn't lose something she packed,
she must have lost
something she bought.
Do you have her address?"
"No, she keeps moving around."
"May I borrow this picture?"
"Sure," Annie said. "Can you find out
why Norway loves Rosamond?"
"I, Nate the Great, would need
a million years to find one clue."
Sludge and I went home.
I got my magnifying glass.
I looked at the photo
Annie got from Rosamond.

I looked at the little figures
in the store window.
They were trolls.
They had very long noses
and hair like a mop.
Hmmm.

Rosamond had written
that what she lost
looked smart like me
and had a very long nose.
I was getting a clue
that I did not like.
Rosamond had lost a troll.
I, Nate the Great,
do not look, think,
or act like a troll.
Actually I did not know
what trolls thought
or acted like.
But I was pretty sure
that they
were not detectives.

They did not eat pancakes
or have a dog named Sludge.
I needed more clues.
"We must go to the library,"
I said to Sludge.
Sludge had to wait outside.
I looked up Trolls.
There was a lot to read.

Most of it was folklore.
I read that trolls live in the
mountains and caves
and under bridges in Norway.
In dark places,
just like Rosamond had written.
They love to eat
all kinds of berries.
They have dark hair
and they never cut it.

I left the library.
Sludge and I walked home.
I had been right about one thing.
Trolls do not eat pancakes.
But I, Nate the Great, do.
At home I made pancakes.
I gave Sludge a bone.

He ate part of it.
Then he took the rest
in his mouth
and went to the door.
I let him out.
He walked around the yard.
I knew what he was doing.
He was looking for
a special place
to bury the rest of his bone.
I ate my pancakes
and thought about the case.
I knew that Rosamond had lost
a tiny troll.
Did she lose it in the palace?
I needed to know more.
I got Sludge.

"Come," I said, "we must
go to Esmeralda's house.
Esmeralda always knows things."
Esmeralda was in her yard
reading a book.
"Esmeralda," I said,
"I am on a case.
Do you know why someone
would take a troll to a palace?"
Esmeralda didn't blink an eye.
She said, "Is the someone
Rosamond?"
"Yes," I said. "I am looking for clues
about her trip."
"Well, I know she was going
hiking in Norway,
and then shopping for presents.
Then she was going to Sweden.

She wanted to see a palace there."
"In that order?"
"Yes. She was saving the palace
for the last part of her trip."
"Anything else?"
"Along the way she was going to
go to smorgasbords
with her cats."

"Have you heard from her?"
"Yes, she sent me her picture
taken in the palace.
She's holding something
with long, dark hair."
"Aha. Trolls have long, dark hair."
"Here's the picture," Esmeralda said.

"I'm using it for a bookmark."
I looked at the picture.
There was Rosamond in the palace.
And she was holding something
with long, dark hair.
Lots of long, dark hair.
My case was solved!
Rosamond had lost
the troll in the palace.
She had written to me
after she had been
in the palace.
She had the troll there
and then she didn't
have it anymore.
Now all she had to do
was get that troll back.

I, Nate the Great, knew that
when Rosamond came home
I would have to tell her
that she had lost the troll
in the palace.
I knew that she would write a card
to the King of Sweden
and ask him to look for the troll
and send it back.
I knew that Rosamond would write
a very strange card.
I, Nate the Great,
felt sorry for
the King of Sweden.
But a case is a case.
"I have solved my case,"

I said to Esmeralda.
"I never thought
that I would solve a case
in a palace."
I looked at the picture
one more time.
There was something about it.

Something in it.

Something tiny, glittering, and green.

Like a cat's eye.

I looked closer.

It *was* a cat's eye.

Rosamond was not holding the troll.

She was holding one of her cats!

I gave the picture back to Esmeralda.

"My case is not solved," I said.

Sludge and I went home.

Sludge went out
to look for his buried bone.
I watched him look.
He could not find it.
He had not been much help
with this case.
It was time for more pancakes.
And more thinking.
What had I learned?
Was there a clue that I had missed?
I had learned from Annie
how Rosamond packed her suitcase.
I had also learned that Rosamond
bought presents.
And I had figured out that
one was a troll.
And that's what she had lost.

But what if Rosamond
didn't *lose* the troll?
What if she *put* it someplace

and forgot?
Where would Rosamond have
put the presents?

In her suitcase, to bring home.
But Rosamond was moving around,
packing and unpacking.
So if she put the troll in the suitcase,
wouldn't she have seen it?
Now, what had Esmeralda told me?
That Rosamond went

hiking
and shopping
and to the palace
and to smorgasbords.

What was important
and what wasn't?
I heard a scratch.
Sludge was at the door
with his bone.
I let him in.
I looked at him and his bone.

Suddenly I knew
what was important
and what wasn't.
I said to Sludge,
"You were trying to help
with the case
when you went looking
for your bone
in a special place.
You were trying to
tell me something."
Sludge wagged his tail.
I said, "I, Nate the Great,
have just solved this case.
Now all we have to do is
wait for Rosamond
to come home."

Two weeks later
my doorbell rang.
I opened the door.
Rosamond and her cats
were there.
She was carrying her suitcase.

"I'm home!" she shouted.
"I came here first
to tell you that
I am still missing
what I lost.
You are a terrible detective.
I knew I should have hired
the King of Sweden."
"How could I let you know
if I solved your case?"
I asked. "I did not know
where you were in Sweden."
"I'm famous in Scandinavia,"
Rosamond said. "I'm easy to find."
"Open your suitcase," I said.
"Why?" she asked.

"You'll see."
Rosamond opened her suitcase.
"See how neat it is," she said.
"I put everything exactly
where it belongs."
"You packed all the presents
you bought?"
"I got T-shirts and a troll,"

Rosamond said. "I packed
the T-shirts
but I lost the troll.
I thought I had packed it,
but it's not in the suitcase."
I bent down to the suitcase.
I picked up Rosamond's hiking boots.
I looked inside the left one.
It was empty.
I looked inside the right one.
Something was in it.
I reached in
and pulled the something out.
It had the longest nose
and more hair than anything
I had ever seen.

"My troll!" Rosamond cried.
"Now I remember where I put it."
"Yes. Annie told me you had
a plan for everything you packed.
You bought this troll
and you gave it a *home*.
You knew that trolls
live in dark places.

So you put it in
the bottom of your boot."
"Right!" Rosamond said.
"It was cozy and perfect."
"And you forgot," I said.
"You had already gone hiking
so you didn't use the boots again.
Time went by.
You went to smorgasbords,
you went to Sweden,
you went to a palace.
Then you remembered that
you hadn't seen your troll.
So you thought you had lost it.
I, Nate the Great, say
that sometimes things
are put in places
that are so special

that nobody remembers
where they are.
Sludge had buried a bone
in a special place
and couldn't find it."
Rosamond clutched the troll.
"Oh, you are so lucky
to be such a great detective.
Because now you can have
the present I got you."
Rosamond pushed the troll at me.
"I am giving everyone else
NORWAY LOVES ROSAMOND T-shirts.
But when I saw this troll
in the window,
I knew it was *you*!"
Rosamond closed her suitcase

and walked out with her four cats.
Sludge sniffed the troll.
"This troll still
needs a good home," I said.
I went down to my cellar,
walked to its darkest corner,
and sat the troll down.
"Enjoy your life," I said.
Then I went upstairs.
This case could have ended better
for me, Nate the Great.

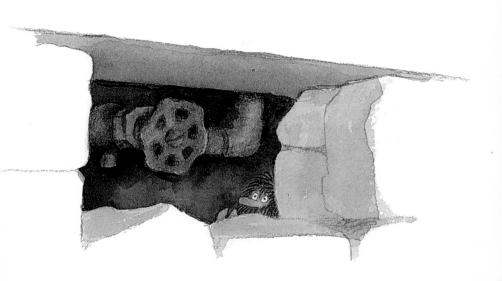

But not for the King of Sweden.
He was one lucky king.
He would never get
a card
or a phone call
or a knock on the palace door
from Rosamond.

DATE DUE

JUN 1 7 1996	
JUN 2 6 1996	
AUG 1 2 1996	